The Dormouse

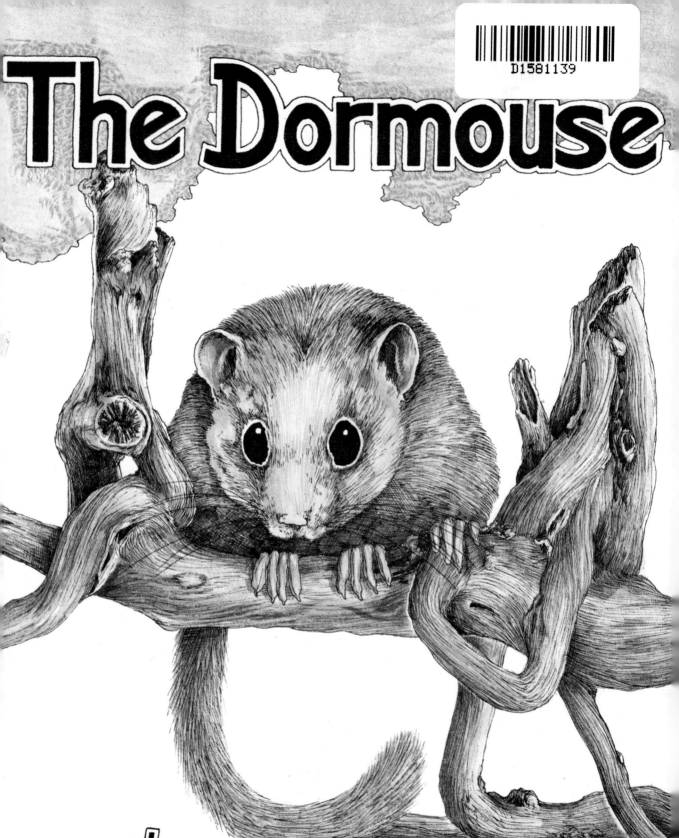

by JOHN HURFORD

For Grandma Brady

Also by John Hurford
ABC OF ANIMALS

First published 1974
Reprinted 1977
© 1974 by John Hurford
Jonathan Cape Ltd. 30 Bedford Square, London WC1

Reproduction by Colourcraftsmen Ltd.,
Chelmsford, Essex
Printed in Great Britain by
Tindal Press, Chelmsford, Essex

Once

there was a

Dormouse

Called

Daffydd

She awoke one spring

When everything was sunny

There were

Daffodils

Primroses

And all sorts of

Flowers

But,

Daffydd was unhappy

So she searched

for a friend

The Voles

were busy **fighting**

The rats were busy gnawing

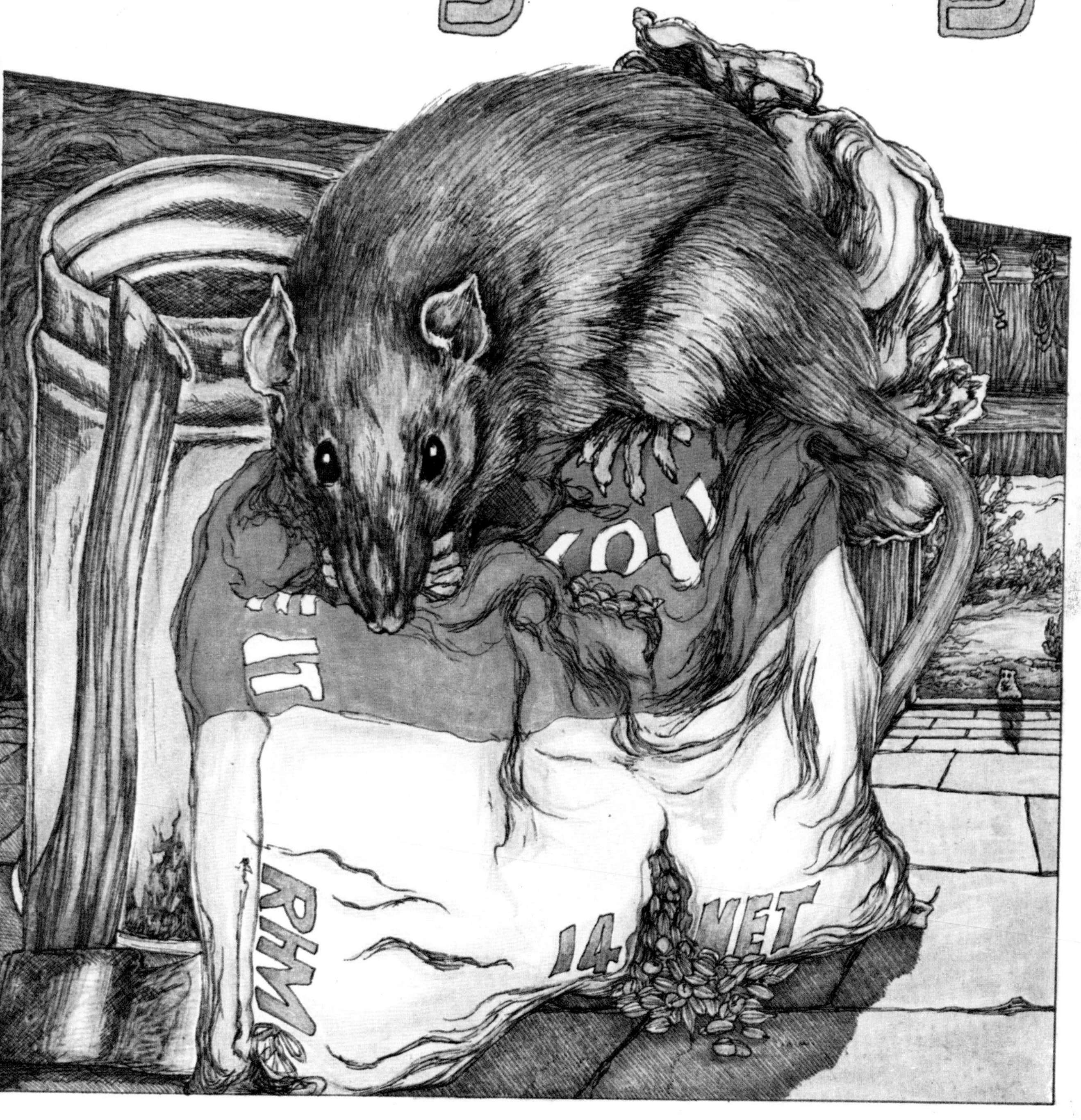

And the Fox

chased her

up a

Rose Bush

She looked into a

Raindrop

And there was a Dormouse just like her

So she climbed through

to meet

her friend

Together they

they

climbed trees

Went into houses

And sometimes

they were frightened

They were both hungry and ate apples and nuts. At last Daffydd decided to go home.

Now she was happy

She knew that whenever she looked into a drop of water there would be her friend looking out at her